THE VERY BUMPY BUS RIDE

RUMBLETOWN BUS

THE VERY BUMPY BUS RIDE

story by Michaela Muntean
pictures by B. Wiseman

Parents Magazine Press • New York

Library of Congress Cataloging in Publication Data.
Muntean, Michaela. The very bumpy bus ride.
SUMMARY: The people, animals, strawberries,
and cream of Rumbletown are given a bumpy
bus ride to the county fair.
[1. Buses—Fiction.   2. Fairs—Fiction]
I. Wiseman, Bernard, ill.   II. Title
PZ7.M929Ve   [E]   81-16905
ISBN 0-8193-1079-4   AACR2
ISBN 0-8193-1080-8 (lib. bdg.)

The Rumbletown Bus stopped
at Number One Bumble Street.
Mrs. Fitzwizzle climbed on board
carrying her prize strawberries
to take to the county fair.

The doors closed with a swish,
and off they went —
bumping and bouncing down Bumble Street.
"My, my," said Mrs. Fitzwizzle.
"This is a very *bumpy* bus ride."

Suddenly the bus bounced to a stop.
HONK, HONK.
The bus driver sounded his horn.
"Honk, honk, yourself,"
answered a gaggle of geese.
"Is this the bus to the county fair?"
"Yes it is," said the driver.

So the gaggle of geese waddled
onto the Rumbletown Bus.

At Number Four Bumble Street,
Mr. Flapsaddle climbed on.
He was carrying two bottles
of fresh cream to take to the fair.
"Good morning," Mr. Flapsaddle said
to a goose nearby.
"Honk, honk," the goose answered.

Then the bus started with a jerk,
and off they went —
bumping and bouncing down Bumble Street.
"My goodness!" cried Mr. Flapsaddle.
"This is a very bumpy, *noisy* bus ride!"

When the bus stopped again,
it was for Granny Smith's pickup truck.
"My truck won't start," Granny said.
"And my cat, Crabapple, and I have a load
of prize apples to take to the county fair."

"Don't worry," said the driver.
"We can tie your truck
to the back of the bus
which is going to the county fair."
"Good idea!" Granny said.

So they tied the truck
to the back of the bus,
and off they went —
bumping and bouncing down Bumble Street.
"Hang on to your whiskers!"
Granny called to Crabapple.

They hadn't gone far
before the bus stopped again.
"Moo-oove!" the driver called to a cow.
"Moo yourself," the cow answered.
"Is this the bus to the fair?"
"Yes it is," said the driver.
So the cow climbed on board.

The last stop was at
Number Six Bumble Street.
Billy McNilly was waiting to take
his pet goldfish, Herbert, to the fair.
Herbert could swim in perfect circles
and Billy was going to enter him
in the pet contest.

They squeezed onto the bus,
and off they went —
bumping and bouncing down Bumble Street.
"Jumping jellybeans!" cried Billy McNilly.
"This is a very bumpy, noisy, *crowded* bus ride!"

Suddenly, the bus stopped again.
But this time it did not stop for a passenger.
It did not stop for a gaggle of geese,
a cow, or a broken-down pickup truck.

It stopped for a hill.
A big, steep hill.

"Everyone out!" the bus driver called.
"We can't make it up this hill."
"But how will we get to the fair?"
Granny asked.

"I'll pull," said the cow.

"We'll push," the others said.

"And we'll honk and let everyone know
we're coming," said the geese.

So they huffed,
and puffed,
and pushed,
and pulled,

and honked,
and mooed,
until finally…

the Rumbletown Bus was on top of
the Bumble Street hill.
And there was the county fair
at the bottom.
"Hooray!" everyone cheered.

But before they could get back on the bus...

it started rolling down the hill all by itself!

"My *bus!*" cried the driver.
"My *strawberries!*" cried Mrs. Fitzwizzle.
"My *cream!*" cried Mr. Flapsaddle.
"My *apples!*" cried Granny Smith.
"*HERBERT!*" cried Billy McNilly.

They all ran after the Rumbletown Bus.
It was rumbling and roaring,
and jiggling and jostling,

and bumping and bouncing
   faster and faster
      down the Bumble Street hill.

Crash! Bang! Clunk! Pop!
The bus stopped right outside
the Rumbletown County Fair.

"Oh, no!" everyone cried when they saw
the strawberries and cream and apples
all over the bus.
And Herbert wasn't swimming
in perfect circles anymore.
He was hopping up and down!

The judges came out to see what had happened.
One judge wiped some strawberries off the bus.
"Mmm ... delicious strawberry jam! First prize!"
And he handed Mrs. Fitzwizzle a blue ribbon.

"This is the best whipped cream
I ever tasted!"
said another judge as she handed
Mr. Flapsaddle a blue ribbon.

Granny Smith won first prize
for her applesauce.
And Billy's fish, Herbert, won the pet prize.
After all, he was the only fish at the fair
that could hop instead of swim.

Everyone clapped and cheered.
Then they all had a wonderful time
at the Rumbletown County Fair.

And it was all because of...

the very bumpy bus ride.

About the Author

MICHAELA MUNTEAN was on a New York City bus one morning when she noticed a woman across the aisle with a full bag of groceries on her lap. "Every time we hit a bump or a pothole," says Ms. Muntean, "that bag would bounce on the woman's lap until finally, things actually fell out and started rolling down the aisle." As Ms. Muntean helped the woman gather her things, her imagination started working. When Ms. Muntean got home, she started writing THE VERY BUMPY BUS RIDE.

Ms. Muntean, who has written many well-loved children's books, lives in New York City. "There are many wonderful things here," she says, "but a bus ride on some of New York's bumpy streets is not one of them!"

About the Artist

BERNARD WISEMAN says that the Rumbletown roads remind him of the roads in his old home town in Connecticut. "Those roads were so bumpy," he says, "that our car once broke down completely after hitting a really big bump."

Mr. Wiseman was a *New Yorker* cartoonist/idea man for many years. His cartoons also appeared in other major magazines, in advertising, and in cartoon books. He left cartooning to start a series of stories for children that were syndicated in Sunday papers across the nation. Then he turned to children's books, and has done more than thirty to date.

Mr. Wiseman now lives in Florida with his wife and children. He is happy to report that the roads are much smoother where he lives now.